HEAT WAVE

ROAD TRIP

HEAT WAVE

ELIZABETH NEAL

DARBY CREEK
MINNEAPOLIS

Darby Creek
An imprint of Lerner Publishing Group, Inc.
241 First Avenue North
Minneapolis, MN 55401 USA

For reading levels and more information, look up this title at www.lernerbooks.com.

Image credits: Master3D/Shutterstock.com, (winding road); MihailUlianikov/Getty Images, (crystals); titoOnz/Getty Images, (sun); John D. Buffington/Getty Images, (girl);PeopleImages/Getty Images, (car); Abstract Aerial Art/Getty Images, (landscape); Ashley Corbin-Teich/Getty Images; (boys).

Main body text set in Janson Text LT Std 12/17.5.
Typeface provided by Adobe Systems.

Library of Congress Cataloging-in-Publication Data

Names: Neal, Elizabeth, 1970– author.
Title: Heat wave / Elizabeth Neal.
Description: Minneapolis : Darby Creek, 2020. | Series: Road trip | Summary: A road trip to the summer's hottest music festival does not go as planned for Marissa, Ben, and T when car troubles threaten to leave them stranded on the side of the road in the middle of the desert.
Identifiers: LCCN 2019004946 (print) | LCCN 2019013500 (ebook) | ISBN 9781541557031 (eb pdf) | ISBN 9781541556874 (lb : alk. paper) | ISBN 9781541572997 (pb : alk. paper)
Subjects: | CYAC: Automobile travel—Fiction.
Classification: LCC PZ7.1.N379 (ebook) | LCC PZ7.1.N379 He 2020 (print) | DDC [Fic]—dc23

LC record available at https://lccn.loc.gov/2019004946

Manufactured in the United States of America
1-46121-43496-6/4/2019

For my parents, who encouraged me
to have adventures

CHAPTER 1

8:48 p.m.

Marissa eyed the clock over the door. Twelve minutes until her shift at Frozen Yo-Zone was over. Twelve minutes until sweet, sweet freedom. She couldn't wait to get out of here. She still had to pack for the music festival this weekend, and T and Ben would walk in any minute.

Marissa narrowed her eyes at the customers still helping themselves to more servings of frozen yogurt and contemplating their toppings. *Just decide!* She beamed the thought to them as loudly as she could, keeping a bright smile plastered on her face.

The yogurt shop was loud and cold. Marissa wished she was allowed to choose the music, but her manager insisted on having cartoons on the widescreen at all times. The cartoons, beanbags, and bright colors were designed to attract young families. But the hum of the yogurt machines meant the TV volume was always set to a roar.

A young couple locked their bikes outside and came in. Melissa winced. *Great,* she thought. *It's almost closing time, people!*

The woman had her hair in braids and was dressed as if she was coming straight from the gym. She loudly remarked on how good the air-conditioning felt. *Not if you've been here for three hours and forty-eight minutes,* Marissa thought to herself. She checked the clock and corrected herself. *Forty-nine minutes.*

The boyfriend was even sportier. He had on a baseball cap, a soccer jersey, and basketball high tops. *How many sports are you bragging about, dude?* Marissa thought. *Pick a lane.*

Out loud she asked, "Hi, can I help you?"

The couple asked if they could sample the

new flavors, and Marissa grabbed some little cups. They used to leave the sample cups out, but now her manager, Paula, made her hide them behind the counter. Paula said the middle schoolers who came every day after school were scamming the system.

Eight more minutes on her shift. Marissa couldn't believe that it was finally happening. That tomorrow night, she, Ben, and T would be three small bodies in the enormous, crowded music festival that took over the desert campgrounds every spring. That she would actually be face to face with Natalia Chavez.

Natalia Chavez was Marissa's favorite singer of all time. She was also the festival's opening-night headliner. The moment Marissa had heard that Natalia was coming to the festival she'd decided she would do anything to see Natalia perform—even camp in a hundred-degree desert with two guys.

The bell over the door jingled again, and Marissa looked up. It was T and Ben. In spite of being exhausted, her face brightened when she saw them. She and Ben went way back:

they'd been friends since kindergarten. They had known each other so long that they fought like siblings.

Ben was the baby of his family, and Marissa had always found him a bit spoiled. After raising Ben's two older brothers, his parents had probably been too tired to hover over Ben. They let Ben do whatever he wanted, a fact that his overall sweet nature only made worse. Marissa thought they'd let him get away with murder. But she and Ben had inside jokes that went back years, so their fights never lasted long. And at the end of the day, he always had her back.

T had joined them in middle school when his family had moved to town for his mom's new job at the hospital. T was a middle child, sandwiched between two sisters. His big sister was a slightly terrifying college student—they tried to steer clear of her whenever she was back in town. She was always yelling at them for playing video games too loudly when she was trying to sleep in. Meanwhile his little sister was eight years younger than T and loved to rope him into tea parties and pedicures. T loved playing board games with his younger sister and video games on his own, especially ones that bordered on the apocalyptic. His sense of humor was a little dark, but as a middle child, he was also good at breaking up tension. He was the glue of their little group, and Marissa was glad that he was coming along.

Marissa gave them a little wave, then turned to focus on three middle-school girls who were ready to be rung up. The girls placed their overloaded cups on the scale and looked at Marissa expectantly for their total.

Marissa smiled at them. They were regulars, so she knew their routine. They biked to the strip mall after dinner sometimes and took turns paying for each other's treats. "That will be $7.83, please," she told them.

The dark-haired girl dug inside her pocket, pulled out a wad of one-dollar bills, and pushed them across the counter to Marissa. Marissa untangled the wad and counted them out one by one, smoothing and organizing the bills as she went.

"Okay, that's six. Do you have one more dollar and eighty-three cents?"

The girls looked at each other, wide-eyed and stumped. The dark-haired girl whispered to the shorter one, "Do you have any more money?"

"I have some change. Let me see . . ." The shorter girl rummaged inside her shoulder bag and poured what she found on the counter.

"How much did you say?" she asked.

"One dollar and eighty-three cents."

"Okay." The shorter girl turned back to the others, looking very serious. "I have four quarters, a nickel, and three pennies. Do you have three quarters?"

Ben fished a dollar bill from his wallet and slapped it on the counter grandly. "Here you go! You can pay it forward someday."

The girls looked at each other, their eyes wide in surprise, and then looked at Marissa, as if they were hoping for instructions from her.

She shrugged and rolled her eyes. "It's okay, I know him. You're good."

"Oh, wow. Thank you, sir!" They grabbed their cups and headed outside, mouths still wide at the unexpected bounty.

Marissa smirked at Ben. "Can I help you, *sir*?"

"Oh, come on, you would have done the same thing."

"Actually, I would have let them work it out themselves," said Marissa. "They like treating each other. But congratulations, hero!"

Ben clutched his stomach and groaned at the direct hit. T laughed and pulled him away by the sleeve. "Come on, let's get our food before she kicks us out."

"That's right, you loiterers!" Marissa grumbled after them. "I've got to ring everybody up before I can clock out." She turned around to smile brightly at the next patrons in line, the sporty couple.

T and Ben grabbed bright paper cups of their own and loaded them up with yogurt and toppings. When they were finished, they came back to the counter.

"Hey, will you give us your discount?" said Ben.

"It's an employee discount, not a friends-and-family discount. If I had that, the whole school would be here every day, claiming to be my best friends," said Marissa. She pointed at the scale for them to weigh their creations.

"Yeah, but we actually *are* your best friends," said T. He grinned hopefully and wiggled his loaded cup at Marissa.

"Mm-hmm. Which is why you're going to be cool and not make this weird, right?" Marissa jerked her head toward Paula in the back, who had moved a little closer when she noticed Marissa talking to people her own age.

T laughed and then nodded his head firmly. "Right."

"Go act like you don't know me so I can finish up here. I have to close out the register and stuff before I can clock out," said Marissa.

T and Ben flopped down at the bright orange booth closest to the cash register. Marissa hummed under her breath as she wiped down the counter. Naturally, though, she kept eavesdropping on T and Ben's conversation.

"It's going to be amazing!" Ben told T. Ben

had gone to the festival last year with his older brother, so T and Marissa had been showering him with questions. "I mean, it does get a little grubby because everybody's camping, but the vibe is really chill. People share their food and everyone takes care of each other."

Marissa couldn't resist calling over, "Be honest, is it a total bro-fest?"

"No! You've seen the lineup. Your hero Natalia is headlining! Do you think she would come if it were a bro-fest?" Ben flashed a giant grin. "Don't worry. We're going to have an amazing time."

"Oh, man, you just jinxed us," T groaned. "We're doomed."

"There's no such thing as jinxes," Ben said breezily, as he spooned out the last bits of frozen yogurt from his giant cup.

Marissa checked the clock again. This final paycheck would cover her food and gas for the weekend.

"All right, you guys, I'm kicking you out! I can't close up until all the customers are gone."

"Okay, okay," said Ben. "We should go

anyway. I told my grandparents we'd swing by after dinner to pick up the car."

Ben's grandparents had an old Honda SUV that they were going to let the three of them borrow for the weekend. Just like his parents, Ben's grandparents also had a hard time saying no to him. Marissa wondered if Ben knew how he had his whole family under his spell.

"Marissa, do you want us to drop you home on the way?" T asked.

"No, I biked over. I'm good. Just, shoo," she said and laughed, making a sweeping motion with her hands. "I'll see you in the morning," she added. "If you want me to have time to pack, let me get out of here!"

CHAPTER
2

9:20 p.m.

Ben pulled up in front of his grandparents'
house and parked along the curb. T peered
out of the passenger window, admiring the tall
pine trees around the tiny lawn. A smaller tree
by the front porch was in full bloom, erupting
bright pink trumpet-shaped blossoms. They
smelled amazing. T loved this time of year.
He could feel the heat of summer building up
during the day, but the nights were still cool
enough to be comfortable.

"Your grandparents' place is so pretty," he
told Ben.

Ben shrugged. "Yeah, I guess so. They've

lived here a long time." He darted across the carefully maintained yard while T took the long way, walking up the driveway and then the footpath to get to the front door. Ben flung open the door, knocking as he did and yelling out to his grandparents, "Grandma, Grandpa? Hiii!" He turned back to T and said, "Come on in, it's fine."

T wiped his feet on the mat and followed him cautiously. "Are you sure they're expecting us?" The house was lit up, but no one was in sight. They could hear dramatic cello music drifting down the hall. T's eyebrows went up. He wasn't about to walk onto the immaculate white carpet without an okay from someone who lived there.

"No, for sure. Grandma said to come by tonight to get the keys. They probably just didn't hear us pull up. Grandmaaaaa!" Ben yelled again. He knocked on the wall as if it were the front door. T heard shuffling noises and then a small but athletic-looking white-haired woman emerged from the back room. She was wearing leggings and a stretchy workout shirt.

"Oh, there you are," she said as Ben leaned over to plant a kiss on her cheek. "I was just starting my yoga DVD. Do you want a snack? I have cookies."

T looked hopeful, but Ben said, "That's okay, we just got frozen yogurt. We just wanted to pick up the SUV. Grandma, you remember my friend T."

"Tiago," T said helpfully. "Nice to see you again, Mrs. Whitcomb. Ben and I were lab partners in biology. Remember we did that science fair project in eighth grade?" T knew that grownups couldn't resist a science nerd. Although he wouldn't mention all of the backyard experiments that he and Ben had gotten into. On more than one occasion, his ER doctor mom had come in handy.

T held his hand out for a handshake, but Ben's grandmother gripped his hands firmly with her hands and held him there so she could study his face. He smiled uncomfortably and shook his curls, making them fall over his forehead and cover his eyes. Protective camouflage.

It didn't work. "The famous Tiago!" she said. "I remember hearing about you and . . . was it Marissa? You two did all the work when Ben couldn't dissect his frog. Isn't that right?" She laughed delightedly.

"Hey!" Ben said, but then shrugged. "I mean, yeah. T and Marissa saved my bacon. What are friends for?" He threw an arm around T's shoulders. Ben's grandmother squeezed T's hand and then released it, turning briskly on her heels.

"Come have some cookies. I need to tell Ben a few things. I have a list . . ." She went into the kitchen. Ben and T followed, exchanging looks. T tapped his wrist, though he wasn't wearing a watch.

"I know," Ben whispered. "But this is the price of borrowing their car."

Ben's grandmother set out a plate of fancy store-bought cookies and gestured toward a bowl of grapes on the counter. Her real focus, though, was clearly The List. She pulled out a pen and a notepad. Ben stretched out his hand for the car keys, but she just tapped the notepad in response. She aimed one perfectly arched eyebrow at him, which made Ben quickly take his seat.

"That's right," she said with satisfaction. "We need to go through this. Now, the first thing. Will you promise me that you'll check the tire pressure before you head out? It's been a while and I'm worried they're a little low."

Ben made his eyes wide and earnest-looking. "Mm-hmm. Definitely."

"Next is gas. You'll bring it back with a full tank, right?"

"Of course!" Ben sounded indignant.

T loaded up a plate with cookies and grapes and settled in for the long haul. He figured there must be at least eight more items on The List.

But Ben was no slouch at this game of wits. He let a giant yawn escape and then, just a little too late, covered it with his hand. He rubbed his cheek and opened his eyes wide, as if he were fighting to keep them that way. His grandmother paused. "Are you tired, sweetie? You need to get a good night's sleep before your long drive."

"No, no, I'm listening," Ben said. "We need to go through the list!"

"Well, yes," his grandmother said. "This is important."

Ben stifled another giant yawn. T almost yawned too from the sheer power of suggestion.

But Ben's grandmother forged on. "Item three: windshield wiper fluid. You need to wash the windshield at every gas stop, and make sure you top off the fluid."

Ben nodded earnestly, rubbing at his eyes.

"Gosh, you two do look exhausted." Her pen hovered over the notepad, tentative.

"I have an idea!" Ben exclaimed, wide-eyed. "Why don't you give me that notepad and I can use it as a checklist, Grandma?"

Checkmate.

Reassured by the earnestness of his request, Ben's grandmother surrendered the car keys. T couldn't help but smile as Ben leaned over to hug his tiny grandmother goodbye.

They bolted out of the house, muffling their cries of victory until they were out of earshot.

The SUV was waiting for them. It was a first generation model, old but well-maintained—not as big as a minivan, not as cool as a Jeep. The car gleamed white under the moon. A black tire cover was mounted on the back.

T whistled appreciatively. "Cool ride!" Then lowering his voice conspiratorially, he said, "Man, I thought we'd have to check the air pressure right in front of her."

"No worries, man. I got you. The trick is to make them think it's all their idea."

"And the tires look fine, right?" T asked, giving them an exploratory kick. They seemed full enough. Of course, he had no idea what he was looking for.

"I'm sure it's fine," said Ben. "She worries. I'll check everything before we head out."

"Cool," T said. "Hey, do you want me to drive your car back to your house?" He gestured to Ben's family car, which was still parked by the curb.

"Nah, my parents will come pick it up tomorrow. Let's go make a playlist for the road trip."

They hopped into the car and T checked out the interior. "Oh, my god," he said. "Is that a cassette player? How old is this car?"

"I mean, it's pretty old." Ben did the math in his head as he adjusted the rearview mirror. "Okay, really old. Like, if it were a person, it could vote."

"Dang," T exclaimed, running his hand over the old-fashioned dashboard controls. "How are we going to play music? I don't have any cassettes."

"Ah-ha, check it out. I bought this thing we can connect our phones to." Ben leaned into the back seat and fished around in his backpack, emerging with a half-opened box. He tossed it at T. "Can you open it up? You plug it into the cigarette lighter . . ."

"This car has a cigarette lighter? Man, that's how you know it's old," T said, cracking up.

"We just have to find a spot on the dial with no radio station." Ben fiddled with the controls, trying to get past all the static. "Okay, so it's going to be hard in town, but it should be no problem once we're out in the middle of the desert. We just have to find a spot where there's no transmission and it will pick up our phone's Bluetooth signal instead. Voila!"

"Oh, that's all, huh?" T was still wrestling with the gadget's packaging.

"Listen, I'm not going to set out across the desert with just an old radio and a cassette player. This thing charges phones too. We're not cavemen." Ben backed up carefully and rolled down the window. A cool breeze swirled through the car, the night air smelling sweet and fresh.

T nodded thoughtfully. "I respect your priorities. And for the record, I've already been putting together an amazing playlist for the trip. But you're not allowed to hear it yet."

"It's not going to be full of old horror movie soundtracks, is it?"

"Hey, that's not a bad idea. Maybe I'll pull together a little something for campfire story time." T gave his best evil laugh, and Ben smiled.

"Hey, don't forget to put some Natalia Chavez on the road trip playlist," he said. "Marissa can't stop talking about her."

CHAPTER 3

10:05 a.m.

Ben pulled up in front of T's house and threw the car into park. The sky was blue and the sun was shining. The day ahead sparkled with possibilities. The road trip, the music festival, no homework, no yard work . . . no work, period. Just three friends in a car, listening to good music. Ben bounded up to the front porch and rang the bell three times. Then one more time, just for fun.

T's dad, looking grumpy and exhausted, came to answer the door. He paused, narrowing his eyes just long enough to make Ben fidget. Then he relented and said, "Hello, Ben."

"Good morning, Mr. Rivera. Sorry about
the bell. I thought . . . um, is T ready?"

T's mom rescued him, her voice singing
out from somewhere deep inside in the house.
"Is that Ben? Ben, do you want some fruit
before you go?"

Mr. Rivera waved him in, holding the door
open. "Come on in. He's ready. His mother
is just concerned he'll starve if left to his own
devices for a weekend."

T's little sister came running to the door.
She was still in her pajamas. "Hi, Ben!"

"Hey, Sofia." Ben mussed up her hair and
she ducked away, wrinkling her nose.

"Stop it, ugh." She smoothed her hair
self-consciously.

"Why are you home? Shouldn't you be
at school?"

"I'm sick," she said cheerfully. "Except
I kind of feel better now so I'm just watching
TV. I was up all night puking though. My dad
is working from home today so my mom can
get some sleep."

Mr. Rivera nodded. "She got called into the

hospital after dealing with all the puking here."

T's mom yelled from the TV room. "Hi, Ben! I can't get up, the dog is comfortable. How about that fruit? Some granola bars?" Ben went over to the living room and poked his head in to say hello. T's mom was still in her scrubs, stretched out on the couch with the family dog draped over her lap like a heavy quilt.

"Hi, Ms. Rivera," Ben said. "Long night?"

She sighed. "The longest."

T appeared in the doorway to the TV room, a big backpack slung on his shoulders. He was wearing shorts, a zombie t-shirt, a fleece hoodie, and slide sandals.

His mom propped herself up on one elbow to talk to them. The dog grumbled in protest. "Tiago, did you get enough breakfast? Is your phone charged? Does Dad know your route?"

"Yes, Mami. We'll be fine, I promise. It's a straight shot. I'll text you when we get there, okay?"

He leaned over to give her a kiss on the cheek and scratched the dog's head. "We gotta go," he said. "Marissa will be annoyed we're getting such a late start."

T's mom slumped back into the couch. "Okay, honey. Drive safe."

***

"Do you know where her new place is?" asked T.

"Yeah, it's not too far," said Ben. "Her mom wanted to make sure they were still in the school district." Marissa used to live in T and Ben's neighborhood, but her mom moved them to a cheaper place when she lost her job last fall. Marissa seemed okay with the move, especially now that all the packing and unpacking was over. She even had her own room now since her older sister had gone off to college.

Ben turned into the parking lot of the condo complex where Marissa and her mom lived.

Beep-beep beeeeeeep!

"Holy Al Pacino," T said. "You're going to get us arrested." He dragged Ben's hands away from the horn before he could press on it again. "Seriously, somebody's going to call the cops. I'm going to the door," said T, and he unbuckled his seatbelt.

But Marissa was already there, waiting for them. She had a giant backpack slung over one shoulder and a sleeping bag in her other hand. Her hair was in one long braid that wound around her head and over her right shoulder. She was wearing her favorite gold sneakers and a floral top. She had been scrolling aimlessly on her phone when they pulled up.

"Does she look mad?" Ben asked T. He honked the horn again as he pulled into the guest parking spot. *Bee-beep-beeeeep.*

T said dryly, "Well, now she does."

Marissa looked up, rolled her eyes, and gave them a *seriously?* face as she walked over.

T jumped out to help her. By the time he got around to the back of the car, she had already opened the hatch and was shoving their stuff around to make room for her bag. The back of the car was cluttered with junk: crumpled receipts, empty shopping bags, a pair of binoculars, an ice scraper, the boys' backpacks, and a grocery bag full of snack food and fruit that T's mom had insisted they take with them. Marissa held up the ice scraper with a quizzical look on her face. "You realize it's going to hit one hundred degrees this weekend, right?"

"Hey, we're ready for anything," said T.

"Ha." She tossed the ice scraper back into the cluttered hatch and lifted up the guys' backpacks to continue taking stock of the inventory. "Did you pack the tent and a cook stove?"

Ben got out and came around back to help with the rearranging.

"Yes to the tent," he said. He patted the vinyl bag into which he had stuffed the tent. "But no, I didn't bother with the cook stove. It's not, like, the wilderness, remember? There will be fancy food trucks and pop-up restaurants and stuff. It's pretty civilized."

"What about extra water? Do we have enough?"

Ben raised his eyebrows. "Don't give me that look," said Marissa. "I know you've done this before, but I've never camped in the desert and I don't want to die of dehydration. It's important to pack extra water."

"Dude. You're not going to die of dehydration. It's only a four-ish-hour drive. And . . . have a little faith in me!" Ben pulled back a tarp to reveal a gallon jug of purified water lying underneath it.

"Yes!" Marissa's shoulders relaxed. "Okay, we got this. I am so excited! Aren't you guys excited? We've been waiting for this all year."

"Very excited," T said. "Also, kinda hungry. Do you want to get breakfast sandwiches? It's not too late for second breakfast, right?"

Ben shrugged. "Never too late for bacon."

"And coffee, please," said Marissa. "I could use another cup. I've been up for hours and all my adrenaline wore off."

"Don't worry, we'll get you caffeinated," Ben said. "Throw your stuff in the back and let's go!"

T lunged for the front seat. "I call shotgun. Mwahaha!"

"Whatever, I don't even care," said Marissa. She threw her bag on top of the heap of stuff before coming around to claim the back seat. "Just gives me more room to spread out."

She poked around in the netting on the back of the seats. "Okay, we're set for sunscreen, apparently." She held up a half-empty bottle. "There are like three of these back here, all different brands. Nothing lower than SPF 30. Plus, bug spray. I love your grandparents. They don't mess around." She popped open a sunscreen bottle and the car filled up with its stale chemical smell.

"Well, if you think about it, they're old white people who live in the desert," said Ben. "The environment is literally trying to kill them at all times. You gotta be prepared." He set up the map on his phone and announced, "Four and a half hours till campsite! We'll be there in plenty of time. We can set up the tent and get some dinner before the show."

"Natalia's act starts at eight, right?" asked T. "Okay, we should be good."

"Yep, and that's just her openers," Ben said. "The lady herself won't be on till later."

He backed out of the parking space and headed for the main road.

"Yes!" Marissa danced in her seat. "You guys, I can't wait. Natalia Chavez is amazing and we are going to See. Her. Tonight! Ahhh!" She grabbed T's shoulders to shake them.

T made a rattling noise like his teeth were going to fall out. "Good lord, lady, settle down." But he was grinning too.

"Can't!" Marissa announced cheerfully. "Won't!"

CHAPTER
4

11:30 a.m.

The traffic along the highway was barely moving. After picking up breakfast sandwiches and coffee, they had zipped through the quiet city and made their way past the suburban strip malls dotted with palm trees. As they left town, the fancy malls gave way to swap meets, and then citrus stands, and then the roadside businesses dried up altogether. Now there was nothing to look at except the cars packed in around them. The land out here was gray and dull, dotted with old billboards, junkyards, and weeds.

The whole car smelled like bacon and fake

syrup and butter. It had been an amazing smell when they were hungry, but the stale aftermath was kind of gross. "I just need one more bacon-egg-and-cheese sandwich," said T, rummaging hopefully through the napkins and greasy wrappers in the takeout bag.

"Well, that's a problem," said Ben, "because we ate them all."

"No!" T groaned. "Why did Past Me think that one breakfast sandwich would be enough?" He held out his t-shirt and inspected all the biscuit crumbs mournfully.

"Past You has no respect for Current You," said Ben, squinting at the road ahead. There was a ton of traffic heading to the festival. They inched along the sun-faded highway.

"Ugh, can't you pass those trucks?" said Marissa. She flipped through photos on her feed, tapping "like" on everything half-heartedly. "It's going to take forever if we're stuck in this traffic all day. I don't want to be setting up camp in the dark."

"Well, what do you want me to do?" Ben gestured at the phone he had clipped to the windshield. Their planned route was bright red and studded with Xs and exclamation marks. "This is the main route. All these cars are probably heading to the festival too."

"Yeah, this is nuts. There has to be another way. Check it out." T held up a frayed atlas. It had been bent open and dog-eared so many times it was barely holding together. "Found it in the glove compartment. Grandparents kicking it old school!"

"Well, yeah. They're grandparents," Ben laughed.

T flipped it open to their state. "I bet I can figure out a different route. What about this little blue road?" He pointed to a tiny squiggle. It would take them a bit north at first, but the route looked like it eventually ran parallel to the freeway.

"Dude, I can't look at that, I'm driving. Show Marissa."

Marissa leaned forward to look at the map. She shrugged. "I'm game. It can't be any slower than this." She settled back into her seat and stared out the window. To keep her hands occupied, she un-did her braid and started redoing it as a fishtail.

"Cool," said T. "So it's settled. Take the next exit and then I'll tell you from there."

Ben, visibly bored, drummed his hands on the steering wheel. The SUV inched forward in the traffic jam. Sun beat down on them like a personal assault.

"So, what do we do in the meantime? I'm so bored," said Ben.

T put his finger in the atlas to keep his place and looked out the window while he thought. "Okay, here's a question: what three things would you take to a desert island?"

"Things, not people or pets?"

"Things," T said decisively. "It's a desert island, you aren't allowed any company."

"Okay, obviously sunglasses. Gotta protect my gorgeous peepers." Ben lowered his head and blinked his eyelashes like Minnie Mouse. "But also a utility knife and a piece of flint."

Marissa snorted from the backseat. "That was a weird combination of vain and practical."

"*You're* a weird combination of vain and practical," he said. "So there. Dude, I'm boiling. Can you turn up the a/c?"

T leaned forward to fiddle with the controls. He said, "It's on full blast, but it's not getting any colder."

"Did you hit the a/c button?"

T looked at Ben without turning his head. "Yes, I'm aware of how air conditioning works."

"No, I'm just saying, because the fan can be turned way up and the dial set to cold but if the little light isn't on . . ."

"Dude. The light is on. See?"

"Hmm. Check your vents." Ben tried flipping his vent dial all the way to the left and then to the right.

Marissa sighed from the back seat.

"You guys, just be patient," Ben said. "It's an old car, maybe it just takes a while to get cold."

Everyone sweltered in silence. They stared out at the bright blue horizon, glittering with an endless row of cars.

1:00 p.m.
"**Y**eah, that's not working," announced T,
putting his hand over the air vent to confirm,
for the fourteenth time, that the a/c was
absolutely, definitely broken.

The car had barely moved because of the
traffic. They had every window open, but
it was hard to tell if that was improving the
situation or making it worse. The sun was
directly overhead now. The air seemed to
shimmer as it rose up from the highway. T
fished a headband from his backpack and used
it to get his hair off his neck.

The truck in the lane next to theirs was

radiating heat off its shiny chrome finish. Marissa shifted uncomfortably in the backseat and rummaged in the seat pockets for something that she could use as a fan. The truck accelerated a little and the noise of the engine rumbled through their car, making it hard for them to hear themselves think.

Ben squinted ahead. "That's our plan B, right?" He put on his signal. The SUV inched forward. The service road appeared through the clump of cars. Escape was in sight.

T sat forward in the passenger seat as if that would give them momentum. Ben sighed with relief as he pulled the SUV off the highway and onto the side road. But instead of slamming on the gas and hightailing it to the campgrounds, he pulled the car onto the shoulder of the road and turned it off.

Ben put the hazards on, popped the hood open, and hopped out.

Marissa looked up from her phone. She and T exchanged alarmed looks. T stuck his head out of the window. "What's going on? Is something wrong with the car?"

No answer.

"Did it overheat?" Marissa groaned. "Oh, my god, this can't be happening."

Ben peeked around the open hood and grinned. "I've got a surprise for you guys. Come see."

T and Marissa unbuckled their seatbelts and got out of the car. The heat rising from the tarmac felt like it was going to melt their sneakers. Somehow it was even hotter out here than it had been inside the car.

Marissa dived back into the car to grab her baseball cap and jammed it on her head before venturing out into the midday glare. She scanned the intersection, trying to get her bearings. They were in the middle of nowhere. The gray dust and gravel was somehow sustaining a single tired-looking tree and a couple of scrubby bushes. A low sign was so sun-faded that she could barely make out the teal lettering that read: "McCoy's Tire Shop: 24 Hour Service." The nearby shop looked like a mobile home that was no longer mobile. It had rusted right into the gravel parking lot. Still, the shop seemed more or less functional: an "Open" sign hung out front, and a clean-ish car was parked in a small lot off to the side.

Marissa and T came around to the front of the car to see what was going on. "Something smells funny," T muttered.

Ben was elbow-deep in the engine, singing under his breath. He emerged, juggling lumps of aluminum foil and blowing on them.

Ben stretched out his arms, proudly presenting the charred lumps to his friends. "Enjoy! I made road food!"

"What?" T started laughing in disbelief. "Are you kidding me? We thought the car had broken down, you jerk!"

"Nope, just a little surprise I had planned. Engine-ladas all round! Well, technically engine burritos, but engine-ladas sounds better."

Marissa said, "Actually, *engi*-ladas sounds better. You're making it weird."

"I'm making it awesome. Engine-ladas!"

Marissa rolled her eyes and grabbed a packet from Ben, juggling the hot foil between her hands. She used the bottom of her shirt as a hot pad and peeled open the top of the foil. She sniffed it suspiciously and then shrugged. "This actually smells pretty good. What's in them?"

"Chicken, beans, and rice. Eat up!"

T made a face. "Dude. That was inside your grandparents' car engine? You know I'm always hungry, but I'm not eating that. You basically cooked it with pollution."

Ben shoved a packet into his hands. "Oh, come on. I double-wrapped them! And they were already cooked—I just used the car to heat them up again. I totally read up on it. You can trust me."

T's stomach grumbled. He had to admit, they smelled amazing.

Ben pressed on. "And it's environmentally friendly! It's not like they were getting dripped on. I can show you where I tucked them. You're just using the excess heat from the car so that it doesn't go to waste." He opened a packet and took a giant bite, as if to prove his point. "See? I'll eat it myself."

Marissa's eyes scanned the horizon. The

sky was streaked with thin, wispy clouds—not the kind that cast any shade. "Today's so hot we could have cooked them on the road."

"Ew, on the ground?" Ben said with his mouth full. "Now *that* would be gross."

T grudgingly tried a bite. "Okay, this is actually pretty good."

"Yes! Told you." Ben licked his fingers with relish and crumpled the extra foil into a ball. He tossed it at Marissa, who caught it one-handed and threw it back at him. Ben ducked and laughed.

Escaping the traffic jam plus eating lunch immediately boosted everyone's mood. They found some rocks to sit on near the scrubby tree and enjoyed their weird roadside picnic. While it wasn't exactly shade, the tree created a dappled effect that gave a little relief from the punishing heat. Marissa walked over to the run-down tire shop and found a functioning vending machine around the far side. She came back with three ice-cold sodas.

She pressed one against her neck before popping it open. "You guys, I can't believe it.

We're actually going to the festival that we've been talking about all year." She passed Ben and T their sodas. "I'm going to see my idol tonight. I heard that on her last tour, she had the entire dance crew on roller skates. Roller skates! One time the dancers had flaming hula hoops."

Ben laughed. "That sounds awesome. I'm excited for the Lonely Swagger Brothers, too. And Beautiful Reason . . . ugh, they have so many good bands in the lineup this year.

T stretched luxuriously and then patted his stomach. "Why is it that everything seems more hopeful with a burrito in your belly?"

"You mean an engine-lada," corrected Ben.

"*Engi*-lada, please, I'm begging you," said Marissa. "Eng-ine-lada hurts my ears. T, back me up, you speak Spanish."

T shrugged cheerfully. "It's a made-up word, Marissa. It doesn't have to make sense."

"Ha!" said Ben. He hopped onto his heels and flung his arms out in glee. "Is it just me or does it even feel a little cooler now?"

"It's not just you. That breeze is saving my

life," said Marissa. She stepped away from the car and glanced at the horizon again. The wispy clouds, in the meantime, had clumped together into a solid mass and looked weirdly dark. "You guys, we'd better get back on the road if we want to get there before dark. How late is it?" There had been no warning of a storm in the forecast, but the look of those clouds was unmistakable.

"It's only, like, twelve thirty," said T. He checked his phone. "Okay, maybe one thirty. But we'll make good time now that we're on the side road. I'm cool with driving the next bit if you guys want. I get to pick the tunes though."

"Uh, no," said Marissa. "Shotgun is the DJ. Everybody knows that."

They dusted the dirt off their shorts and got back in the car, ready to knock out the next leg of the trip. The wind swirled around them, sending up clouds of dust and tumbleweeds. The skies ahead loomed darkly as they pulled back onto the road.

CHAPTER 6

2:00 p.m.

"So much for beating the storm," said T as he squinted through the gray wall of water in front of them.

"It feels like the storm is beating us," said Marissa. "It's literally battering the road."

The skies had opened up and thunder rolled across the desolate open land. Rain lashed down on them in sheets, and water bounced off the car's roof like marbles. They could barely hear each other over the radio and the rhythmic thump of the windshield wipers. Marissa leaned forward and turned off the music so she could think.

T gripped the steering wheel tighter and leaned forward in his seat. "I can barely see where I'm going, you guys." He kept rolling a toothpick from one side of his mouth to the other and then back again.

Ben leaned over the back of Marissa's seat and winced. The pounding rain hid the road completely. "Should we pull over for a little bit?"

"We don't really have time for another stop after all the traffic we hit this morning," said Marissa.

Ben scooted forward so he could reach the dashboard. He pushed the hazard lights on, and Marissa looked at him. "You are such a backseat driver!"

"Just in case," he said. "Not that anyone's really on this road, but that would be just our luck, to have some big truck come barreling down on us . . ."

"Oh, my god, shut up!" said Marissa. "You're freaking me out." She reached and tried to hit his arm, but Ben ducked back into his seat.

T stared at the sheets of water coursing down the windshield. The car's wipers were barely keeping up. He veered a little to avoid a giant puddle along the side of the road, sending up a huge arc of water as they plowed through.

All of a sudden, every phone in the car started blaring.

T yelped. "What in the Denzel Washington is going on?"

Marissa picked up her phone from her lap and read the alert. "Flash flood warnings. Yikes." She silenced her phone, but the angry red warning continued to flash on her screen.

T slowed down to forty-five miles per hour. "Any trucks behind me are just going to have to deal." Still, he braked a little every few minutes to light up the taillights, and kept checking the rearview mirror nervously.

"This is freaky," he said. "Hey, do you remember in that show where there's a storm, and the guy looks out the window and sees a freaky ghoul messing with the engine?"

"Stop," said Marissa. "Anyway, wasn't that a plane?"

"Yeah, you're right," said T. "But doesn't it feel like we're moving into a land of both

shadow and substance, of things and ideas?"
He lowered his voice ominously. "We may have
just crossed over into . . . the Twilight Zone!"

Marissa groaned in reply, but she also
started laughing. She fell quiet and bit the
inside of her cheek. "Ugh, you guys, what if we
don't make it in time for Natalia? What if the
road is washed out ahead? I wish we'd stayed on
the freeway."

"I guarantee it's raining there, too," said
Ben. "You have to chill. There's nothing we
can do right now except try to drive safely."

"Which is what I'm doing. Jesus." T
tightened his grip on the steering wheel
and shook his head. "Would you guys stop
distracting me?"

"I'm sorry. I'm just stressed," said Marissa.
"I've been working all year for these tickets,
and seeing Natalia means a lot to me. You guys
don't know . . ."

"Marissa, enough already," snapped Ben.
"We can't control the weather. Let him
concentrate on driving. I still think we should
pull over. This is crazy."

Marissa checked the side of the road. The water beside the car ran brown and fast. "Honestly, I don't think there's anywhere to pull off. At least if we stay on the road we're on high ground. The water is rising really fast."

T risked a quick glance at Marissa. He could see that she was genuinely upset. "Look, there's no way they're letting acts go onstage in a storm like this. Probably the whole show will be delayed. Maybe they'll even reschedule her for tomorrow."

"At this rate, we won't even make it by then." Marissa groaned again. "I knew taking this side road was a stupid idea."

"What?" Ben's voice was high and indignant. "You never said anything—"

Crack. Boom!

A lightning bolt sliced the sky in two, setting the dark underside of the clouds ablaze for a split second. It felt like the lightning had struck just a few inches away from the car. A deep roll of thunder made their chests vibrate and lifted the hair on the back of their necks.

"Oh, my god," said Ben. "Seriously, should we pull over? I don't want to wreck my grandparents' car." The rain was now bouncing off the windshield like bullets. *Tat-a-tat-tat-tat.*

"I can't even see the shoulder," said Marissa. "There's water right up to the edge of the road and we have no idea how deep it is. Are there any exits coming up?"

Ben checked the map. "Not for, like, five miles."

"You guys, I'm kind of freaking out," said T. "I can barely see the road. What if someone comes up behind me?"

Flash. Once again, a bolt of lightning lit up the sky behind them.

"Jeez! That almost gave me a heart attack!" T grabbed his chest, trying to catch his breath. He swerved to miss a deep pool of water on the road. "Ooh, I just thought of something," he said suddenly. "Next time we see lightning, start counting."

Another bolt flashed. "Okay. One Mississippi, two Mississippi, three Mississippi, four . . ."

Marissa and Ben held their breath, bracing for the next roll of thunder.

". . . six Mississippi . . ."

Thunder rumbled again in the distance. Marissa looked at T expectantly. He did some mental calculations and then answered the unspoken question. "It's 1.2 miles away now."

"That's still pretty close," said Marissa.

"Better than before, though," said Ben. "Maybe the storm is moving through."

Marissa lifted an eyebrow at the wall of water still pounding the road.

But for once, Ben's optimism proved well-founded.

The sky started to lighten up, and the storm was over almost as quickly as it had rolled in. The rain gradually lessened and the dark clouds lost their glower. The road and its shoulder were still filled with puddles, but at least T could now see and steer around them. Steam rose from the road in wobbly spiral towers.

"This is almost as spooky as the storm," said Marissa. But she felt herself relaxing, and the warnings had disappeared from their phones. They drove through the rising steam in quiet for a few minutes.

"Let's open up the windows again," said Ben. "Maybe the rain cooled things off."

But if anything, the brief storm had left things more tropical than before. They felt the air, still roughly a million degrees, settle back over them. Marissa checked the clock.

"Three twenty-eight," she said. "We can still make it in time."

CHAPTER
7

4:00 p.m.

It was sweltering in the car, but the skies were clear and their spirits were high again. They still had a half tank of gas and a full bag of snacks. Ben had broken into the fruit that T's mom had packed and was already on his second banana.

T glanced at the GPS on his phone. "Hey, somewhere in that storm we crossed the state border and didn't even realize it. We're over halfway there!"

Marissa offered to take over the wheel.

"Nah, I've only been driving for a little while," said T. "I'm doing okay."

"Yeah, but that was like a lifetime in terms of stress," said Marissa. "You could just pull over real quick and we can switch. Why don't you take a break?"

T hesitated.

"Don't try and be macho about this," said Marissa.

"Ha. Fine." T signaled and steered the car onto the gravel shoulder. It was still muddy and there were puddles everywhere. He sighed and stretched his neck to either side. He had to admit, it did feel good to stop. "All right, let's do this." He checked behind him, then cracked the road-side door open and slid out.

Marissa flung her door wide and hopped out too. T was doing jumping jacks. She laughed at his hair bobbing in the breeze and his sneakers squelching in the mud.

"Hey, it feels good to move!" T said. "You should try it." He kept bouncing up and down, his hair bouncing along with him. "Come on! Gimme twenty!"

Marissa looked down at her shiny gold sneakers and then back up at T. She shook her head. "Dude, you're not my drill sergeant." She hip-checked him on her way into the car. "Let's go! We've got a concert to see."

Marissa slid the seat forward and adjusted all of the mirrors. T watched the whole routine with a bemused look. "Dang, Marissa," he said. "I knew you were short, but this is ridiculous."

"Hey!" She checked the time on her phone. "Focus, people. We can still make the campsite before it gets dark. Maybe we'll even have time for dinner."

"You know they always start these things late," piped Ben from the back seat. "It'll be at least an hour before whatshername actually comes on."

"Show some respect, man. This is Natalia Chavez, Queen of the Live Show, First of Her Name, Breaker of Billboard Records, Dropper of the Mic."

T and Ben looked at each other, stunned into silence.

"Yeah, that's right," said Marissa. "Anyway, I'm just saying . . . you said there were food trucks, right?"

"Yeah, there were some pretty good options last year," said Ben.

"I'm getting hungry again," T moaned. "Can you pass me the fruit bag?" Ben tossed it forward.

"Dude, how much did you eat?"

Ben shrugged. "Sorry. I was bored and it was there!"

Marissa pulled back onto the road, her back wheels spraying gravel. "I hope you're buckled in, gentlemen," she said. "I'm driving to make up for lost time."

"Yesssssss!" T yelled.

Ben shook his head. "Whoa, there, Leadfoot! This is my grandparents' car, remember?"

"I am not missing a second of Natalia's show," said Marissa, twisting her head around to face him. "I cleaned frozen yogurt tubes all year for this."

Ben winced. "Yeah, I don't like thinking about the tubes."

"It's not fun to think about," said Marissa. "It's also not fun to get in there with the brushes, scraping gunk out of the hoppers . . ."

Ben plugged his ears with his fingers. "La la la, I can't hear you. Frozen yogurt is *frozen*, so it's magically safe forever."

Marissa spoke louder. "And then you have to flush the sanitizer through, three times, draining out the milky liquid and clumps . . ."

"Stop ruining frozen yogurt! Quick, T, put on some music."

"Dude, yes. I just have to charge my phone." T leaned over to take Marissa's phone off the cord, but the cord resisted his grip. He gave it a hard, quick yank and the cord, already old and frayed, broke off in his hand.

Marissa gasped. "What did you do?"

"I don't know!" T yelped. "I was just trying to plug my phone in so I could play you guys my road trip playlist. Let me see if I can fix it."

Marissa forced out a breath, trying hard not to blow up at him. T shone his phone's flashlight onto Ben's gadget's USB port, where the cord's plug was firmly stuck. From the end of Marissa's cord, frayed wires were sticking out, too short to grab them safely.

"Are you kidding me?" said Marissa, seeing

the damage. "Does anybody have tweezers? Duct tape? Or, um, another music-charger thingie?"

"Uh, no," said Ben. "I only brought that one. The one T just broke."

"Oh, come on. It's not broken—it's just Marissa's janky cord that broke. We'll get it out," said T, and checked the rear-view mirror to gauge Ben's expression.

"I don't know, man. It looks pretty broken." Ben exhaled a long, frustrated sigh. "Should we just put the phone in the cup holder?"

"I'm sure we can find something on the radio . . ." T flipped frantically through the stereo buttons, until Marissa swatted his hand away.

She pushed the "seek" button a few times. The only sounds that came through were staticky preachers, hyperventilating talk radio hosts, and crackly old country songs.

"Holy cannoli," T said. "We're in the middle of flipping nowhere." He scanned the desert horizon nervously, as if the lack of music had made him realize just how isolated they were. For miles there had been no houses, no businesses—just a couple of lonely saguaros. "Seriously, first no a/c and now this? Worst road trip ever."

Marissa gave him a look that could have melted steel. "Maybe you should have thought of that before you yanked the cord!" She squinted into the western sun and adjusted her baseball cap a little lower. They all sat quietly, simmering.

"I could sing," Ben offered. He cleared his throat and started warbling, "What would you do, if I sang out of tune?"

Both Marissa and T snapped, "No!" in unison. They drove on in angry silence.

CHAPTER
8

5:00 p.m.

The sun was sinking lower in the sky, painting the dusty hillsides with rose, orange, and purple. The empty grazing areas that before had looked lonesome and barren were getting a gorgeous makeover. Each scruffy, undignified bush cast an elegant, elongated shadow. The saguaros on the crest of the hill looked like towering giants.

Though the late afternoon light was lavish and spectacular, everyone was too irritated to admire it.

Soon T noticed a competing electric glow just off to the south. He checked their progress against the atlas and then the map on his phone. He looked up again, suddenly beaming. "You guys, do you see that? I think those might be lights from the festival! We're almost there!"

"Seriously? Oh, thank god." Marissa pressed her foot on the gas, newly energized. The air in the car swirled around them and the edges of the atlas fluttered in the breeze.

And then there was a loud *FOOMP* . . . *whoosh!*

One of the wheels was thumping loudly, the loose rubber whacking the road with every rotation. *Fwack, fwack, fwack, fwack!*

The car shook violently and everything was loud. Marissa couldn't think. All she knew was that this wasn't good. Something told her she wasn't supposed to slam on the brakes. She took a deep breath and clutched the steering wheel tightly, trying to prevent the car from pulling them off the road.

Ben and T were both yelling.

"Hold tight, slow down!"

"Did you run over something?"

"I don't know!" said Marissa. "I think it's one of the tires. I've gotta pull over."

T braced his feet against the dashboard. Ben was leaning forward. "Slow down! Get off the road!"

Marissa tried to brake, but that made the car lurch even more. She switched back to the gas, giving it a little pump to get the car back where she wanted it. She flicked on the right-turn signal, eased off the accelerator, and exhaled in relief as the car responded. They began to slow and she steered gently to the side of the road so they could figure out what the heck had just happened. The car bucked and bumped over the ground.

A yellow sports car zoomed up out of nowhere, veering around them into the oncoming lane. The driver laid on his horn angrily and yelled at them as he zipped past. Ben and T yelled rude things at him, suddenly loyal to Marissa now that someone else was honking at her.

Finally, after an eternity, the SUV rumbled to a shaky stop on the side of the road.

They all sat there for a second, stunned. Even the car felt off-balance, slumped in defeat.

Marissa was still clutching the steering wheel, trying to slow her breath before she trusted herself to let go. T sat frozen in his seat—still braced for a crash, feet up against the dashboard. Marissa exhaled hard and then, to everyone's surprise, started giggling. T looked over at her, and she shook her head helplessly. "I can't . . . I'm sorry," she gulped, trying to explain. She was shaking with laughter.

T snorted. He and Ben started laughing, uncomfortably.

"It's not funny," Ben said weakly from the back seat.

"I know! It's not funny at all!" Marissa was laughing so hard she could barely get the words out.

T just said, "Marissa." He was grinning, but like he felt wrong about it.

Marissa was clutching her stomach. "Oh, god, it hurts." She straightened, gasping for breath. "Okay. Phew. Pull it together."

She rubbed her eyes and flicked on the hazards. "Let's go see what happened."

***

Outside the car, the residual heat and steam rising from the gravel quickly warmed their legs. The air still smelled like rain and felt electrically charged from the storm.

"I think it came from the back," said Marissa. "Let's go look."

Sure enough, the back right tire was shredded. It had peeled halfway off the tire rim.

"Jeez, Marissa," said Ben. "You really did a number on it."

Marissa's mouth fell open. "Excuse me? How is this my fault?"

"I'm just saying. You were driving pretty fast."

"I was going the speed limit! On a wet road that was covered in random debris from the storm. It could have been anything." She glared at Ben.

"Hey, I didn't mean anything by it. I'm just freaked out." He shot T a desperate *help-me* look.

Marissa's voice rose. "How do you think I feel? I was the one driving. Now your grandparents are going to think I broke their car." She tugged angrily at her hair tie and pulled her fishtail out. She walked away from the car to catch her breath, combing her fingers through her hair to redo it into a high ponytail.

T surveyed the empty roadside. The scrubby trees loomed over them, seemingly doubled in size, their shadows getting longer by the minute. "And of course now nobody's driving by that we could flag down for help," he said. "That guy was such a jerk. Couldn't he see we had car trouble?"

Nobody answered him.

"Man," he went on. "This place is kind of creepy. It feels like a zombie could come lurching over those hills any minute." He pulled his shoulders up by his ears and shivered, but his eyes twinkled with excitement.

"Oh, my god," said Marissa. "You're loving this, aren't you? You are such a weirdo." She turned to Ben, shaking her head. "Okay.

Can you call roadside assistance?"

Ben looked blank. "I don't know if my grandparents have that."

"Wow, I thought you guys had everything."

"Hey, that's not fair."

Marissa sighed. "I just meant I thought that was a thing all grownups had."

"Well, I don't think they do." Ben avoided her eyes. "They've never needed it, I guess. They mainly just use the car around town."

T tugged on Marissa's sleeve to get her to stop glaring at Ben. "Look, we don't need roadside assistance. It's just a flat tire. We can change it ourselves and still make it to the show on time. We have a spare, right?"

"Uh, yeah," Ben said. "It's right on the back of the car, remember?" He pointed at the big covered wheel mounted there.

"Okay. So, just . . . everybody relax," said T. "We'll get this changed and be back on the road in no time. Ben, why don't you look up where the closest auto shop is? Then we can get an actual replacement tire before the drive home."

Ben wandered off, looking for a signal. Meanwhile, Marissa and T uncovered the spare tire. T started laughing when he saw how it compared to the three good tires. "This looks like a toy," he said, poking it.

Marissa eyed it skeptically. "Yeah, well, I guess it only has to get us to civilization. Can you go look in the glove compartment for a manual? We're going to need a wrench or something, too, to unscrew this wheel."

T tossed the manual to Marissa and started unscrewing the spare from the back door.

Marissa read through the directions and started working through the steps. "Okay, first we have to put on the parking brake. I'll do that." She hopped back into the driver's seat to set the brake, and then sat down with the manual, reading the next bit.

Ben reappeared, holding up his phone. "The closest one is that McCoy's place, miles behind us. Too far to walk. But," he announced, "I found this article on how to change a tire safely."

Marissa held up the car manual.

"All right, well, I'm just saying . . ." He trailed off sheepishly. "Okay, fine. What's the next step?"

"It says we have to find something to brace the wheels opposite the blown tire. Like bricks, or a rock, or a heavy log or something."

"That's what my article says too," Ben began, but T shot him a warning look.

Marissa raised an eyebrow and kept going. "Do you guys want to look for something heavy? I'll get the jack and stuff out of the back. It looks like we're going to have to unpack the entire backseat to get at it." She clasped her hands behind her head and blew out her breath. Her face was flushed from the heat. She got out, walked around to the back, and flung open the hatch. Without another word, she started throwing their bags onto the side of the road as fast as she could.

"Should we . . . help you?" Ben offered lamely, but Marissa shooed them away.

"Go!" she said. "Find heavy things! I got this."

Ben and T headed out into the twilight on

their mission. They climbed down into the
gulley by the side of the road, jumped over a
little drainage creek, and crawled through the
slats of a dilapidated metal fence into an open
field. Though the sun was sinking lower, the
day had not released its heat.

Slowly, they began picking their way
through the field. T used his phone as a
flashlight, scanning the area from side to side
in the hopes of catching the shadow of some
promising rock or log. Ben elbowed T's side.
He began, "So, don't tell Marissa but . . ."

"But what?"

"Well, when I was going to search for the
nearest auto shop, I did something else first. I
looked up why blown tires happen." He looked
over at T and screwed up his face like he was
bracing for a hit.

"And?" T eyed him. "You were looking
for more ammunition against her? That's not
cool, man. I gotta tell you, sometimes you and
Marissa's frenemy thing gets old."

"No," Ben said. "I mean, okay, maybe. But
actually I was feeling guilty about this." He

fished a crumpled piece of paper out of his jean pocket and unfolded it: his grandmother's list.

"Uh-oh," said T. He reached for the list and shone his phone light to read it more closely. None of the boxes were checked off. T started to laugh. He swatted Ben on the head.

"Yeah," Ben said. He rubbed his head ruefully. "So, one of the things I didn't do was check the air pressure. And, well. Guess what causes blown tires?"

"Let me guess: high air pressure?"

"No, *low* air pressure, actually." Ben sighed. "Turns out my grandma wasn't just being a worrywart."

They stood there awkwardly, thinking to themselves.

"So, in other words, it had nothing to do with Marissa driving too fast," T said.

"Yeah. And everything to do with my not checking the air pressure." He kicked a rock over the sand. "So, what should I do?"

T laughed. "I don't know, apologize? Or, just, like, don't be an automatic jerk next time?"

"Hey!" Ben aimed a kick at him and T

dodged it, leaping over something that almost tripped him up.

"Oh, check it out. Big rock!" T pointed the light from his phone at a rock about the size of Ben's head. It was perfect. They found another not long after.

They came back in triumph, hoisting the stones high over their heads like trophies.

Marissa was sitting on the back bumper, surrounded by the mess of their belongings strewn about. She had a small jack in her left hand and the car manual in the right. Glancing up from the manual, she said, "Yeah, those'll work. Shove 'em under the front wheels."

"Hey, a little celebration, please?" said Ben. "It is surprisingly hard to find decent-sized rocks out here."

"Oh, sorry." Marissa slow-clapped. "My heroes! Thank you! Well done!"

"Okay, that feels less than genuine," said Ben. T shot Ben a warning look, and Ben changed tactics. "But I'll take it. And you're welcome."

"I have never been so hot in my life. And I'm hungry again." T rubbed his stomach and looked at Ben. "I don't suppose you have any more burritos hidden in the engine?"

"I wish. I might have some cheese puffs, though . . ." Ben began digging through their bags.

Marissa held out the jug of water, now warm from the day's heat, and said, "Here, at least drink some. But stay focused. We've got a concert to get to."

They kicked the rocks into position under the car's front wheels, then got on the ground to try and place the jack.

"I think it needs to go back a little," said Ben. Marissa had her finger in the car manual, marking her spot. She flipped it open again and showed him the diagram.

"Fine. You're right." He pushed himself back to his feet.

Marissa cranked the car up until the blown tire was hovering an inch above the ground.

"Okay, that's good, stop!"

"Great," said Marissa. "Now we get the lug nuts off, right?"

They popped the hubcap off and tried

to screw off the lug nuts. Ben grunted with the effort.

"Ugh, they're tight."

"Let me try."

All three tried in turn, but the lug nuts would not budge. It was as if they were welded into place. Ben put the wrench back on and tried stomping on the handle with one foot. Nothing.

He grabbed the car roof as if to put his full weight on it with both feet, but T pulled him away. "Whoa, that doesn't look safe," T said. "Let's lower the car again, to give ourselves more traction."

Ben looked embarrassed, but agreed. They spun the jack down until the car's full weight rested on the tires again.

"Let's do this," said T. He flexed his muscles and gave a dramatic roar.

"All right, Thor, have at it," said Marissa, rolling her eyes.

But the lug nuts still wouldn't turn.

"Man. It feels like they're rusted in place," said T. "Do you have any of that stuff? The squirty thing your dad uses on everything?"

Ben shook his head slowly as he scanned the tray of tools Marissa had set in the dirt. "I don't think so." He kicked a duffel bag in frustration. "This is so stupid. We're stranded here because these stupid lug nuts won't move!"

Marissa grabbed the wrench. "Let me try again."

She tried every single lug nut in turn, but all of them were equally stubborn. After several minutes of trying and grunting, Marissa finally threw the lug wrench to the ground.

"I can't believe it," she said, sounding on the edge of tears. "All this for a show we're not even going to see."

CHAPTER
9

6:00 p.m.

They dispersed in the gathering gloom to cope in their own ways. T was trying to look up how-to videos, but was having trouble getting a signal. He wandered up and down the side of the road, holding his phone out at different angles to try to find some bars.

Ben sat on the ground, leaning against the car and staring blankly into space. Every so often, he looked over at Marissa. But each time, he shook his head. He didn't know how he could confess now, after everything that had happened.

Marissa was still trying with the lug wrench. She kept muttering and swearing under her breath. Occasionally, she took a break to take a nervous slug of water from the gallon jug. Finally, she flung herself down next to Ben and pulled out her ponytail so she could rest her head against the car. They stared out into the desert, legs pulled up in a huddle. Marissa checked her phone for a signal, but there was none. The sun was setting.

"We're going to die out here," she said. "They're going to find our bones."

"We're not going to die," said Ben. "Someone will come and give us a ride. Eventually."

"*Eventually* doesn't help when Natalia Chavez is stepping onstage at 8. At this point, I'd even be happy to see that jerk in the sports car."

To pass the time, they reverted to arguing about whose fault it was.

"If we were on the main highway, I guarantee you someone would have come along to help by now," said Marissa.

"I'm just saying," said Ben, "If you go too fast on a hot road, on under-filled tires, you're basically asking for trouble!"

"I was not going too fast! And what do you mean, under-filled tires? How can this be my fault when it's your family's car?"

"Never mind." Ben fidgeted. "Can you pass me the water?"

T came back to the car, still focused on his phone. Ben looked up, relieved for the distraction. "Did you find anything?"

"Nope," said T. "But I do have a plan." He pressed a button on his phone and the tinny sound of a trumpet swelled up in the desert air. A beat kicked in and the bass dropped. T started to nod his head, his curls bobbing to the beat and his shoulders moving along.

Confused, Ben and Marissa looked at each other. Marissa looked up at T, who was full-on dancing now, swaying from side to side as he held his phone aloft. She thought, not without affection, that he looked like an idiot. An idiot who was having fun.

Marissa strained to hear the music from his phone. "Is that Natalia?"

"Her first hit! This is the mix I was trying to play for you guys. Come on." He gestured for her to join him. "Come on! We're not getting anywhere on this tire. We need a dance break. If we can't make it to the concert, we'll have our own." He put the phone on the top of the car and held out his hands to the both of them. Marissa and Ben exchanged another look. Ben shook his head a little. Marissa read it: *this is weird.* That was all she needed to decide it was actually awesome. She slapped her hand into T's and pulled herself up.

"Yes!" he shouted with glee. T twirled Marissa around and sent her spinning into the gravel by the side of the road. She tried to recover her cool and her balance, but it was too late for both. All the tension of the day came rolling off her shoulders, and she danced it into the dry desert night. She laughed and called back to Ben. "Come on, Ben. Don't be a holdout. You know you want to dance."

T took up her entreaty and turned it into an exuberant chant. "You know you want to dance, get up and shake your pants! You know you want to dance . . ."

Marissa put her hands on his shoulders,

creating a mini conga line, and they conga-ed back and forth in front of Ben.

T and Marissa started jumping up and down to their own lyrics, their beat superimposed on to the music still drifting over their heads. Marissa shouted, "¡Baila, baila!" and T swung back around toward Ben. Ben groaned, but he took T's outstretched hand to join the conga line. Marissa threw her head back and laughed. "Now we just need roller skates!"

"I prefer hula hoops," Ben said.

"You guys. What if Natalia notices our amazing dance moves and pulls us onstage? She actually does that sometimes." Marissa's eyes gleamed in the darkness, imagining their hypothetical moment of glory.

T laughed. "I don't know if our conga line is going to cut it. We need to work up a better routine." He broke away and started doing the robot.

"Or, a *robot* conga line," said Marissa.

Ben stopped dancing so that he could strategize. "No, we need to do something really cool, that she can actually see from the stage. Marissa, let's go." He held out his hands as if he was bracing himself to catch her.

She raised one eyebrow, and shook her head. "No way. You're going to drop me."

"No faith! I'm hurt." Ben turned to T. "Okay, man. Let's do this."

T nodded. He took a running start and jumped into Ben's arms shouting, "Use your knees!" Ben staggered backward under his weight, but managed to spin him around awkwardly before they both fell into the gravel, cracking up.

Marissa clapped. "Nice form. I really felt your connection. I think you need a bit more height, though."

"He's too big to lift," Ben said. "I can't get any leverage."

T jumped up and dusted his hands. "All right, Marissa, we need you in the mix."

"Ha! I'm game as long as I'm not the one getting thrown around."

Ben and Marissa assumed a lunge position, facing each other, and T carefully climbed up on their knees. Bracing himself against their shoulders, he steadied himself, and then raised his arms triumphantly.

"Oh, my god, that's it!" Marissa stood up abruptly and T tumbled to the ground.

Ben nodded with satisfaction. "Yep, I think we got it that time."

"No, about needing leverage—that's *it*!"

The guys looked at each other, confused. But Marissa's face had lit up. "We gotta look in the trunk again," she said, lunging for the hatch door.

"For what?" Ben asked. "We already emptied everything out—hey, what are you doing?"

Marissa had peeled back the mat again and was checking the side compartments.

"Would your grandparents have a pipe in here?" she said finally.

Ben looked indignant. "They don't smoke."

"Oh, my god. Not a smoking pipe. A pipe-pipe. Like, for plumbing. Something long and metal?"

"Why would they have a pipe in the trunk?"

T's face lit up. "I get what you're saying.

We need to extend the wrench, to put more counterweight on the lug nuts."

Marissa nodded. "Exactly."

They scoured the car. T pulled out the ice scraper. "Hey, what about this?"

"Does the brush part come off?"

They tugged and twisted at it for a while but it was solid plastic, and useless.

Ben kicked along the side of the road and found a long stick in the gulley, but there was no way to attach it to the wrench. It snapped as soon as they put weight on it.

They needed something sturdier. Marissa spotted a mile marker's reflector strip gleaming as it caught the light from their phones. "You guys, I have an amazing idea."

CHAPTER 10

7:00 p.m.

The three friends grunted with their effort, but the mile marker remained stubbornly planted in the ground. "Move, will you!" Marissa yelled, kicking at it in frustration.

"Wait, is this illegal?" T pulled back, wiping sweat away from his forehead. "It feels illegal."

Ben shrugged. "Just a little. Don't worry, though—my parents are lawyers. They'll get us off the hook."

T cocked his head to one side, trying to figure out if Ben was serious.

Ben sighed. "Yeah, it's probably illegal.

But more to the point, it's also impossible. This thing hasn't budged an inch."

T put a hand on his arm to pull him away. "We should look around a little more. Wasn't there some fencing along that drainage ditch we crossed?"

Ben turned to scan the horizon. "Yeah, I remember. You think we can knock something loose there?"

"Worth a shot," said Marissa. "Easier than getting this out of the ground, anyway."

Ben and T led Marissa back to the bottom of the gulley. They found the sad, rusted suggestion of a metal cattle fence. T kicked it experimentally, and the whole thing vibrated like a tuning fork.

"Yes!" he said. "That means they're hollow, right?" He grabbed and wiggled the different pipes and posts like he was playing a high-stakes game of Jenga. "What about this one? I think it's the loosest," he said. "If we could push this post over a little, I bet we could kick one of the pipes free. What do you guys think?"

Ben gave it a push. "Oh, yeah, that's going

to work. How about you shove the post, and Marissa and I will kick on three. Ready? One, two, *three!*"

T shoved with all his might while Ben and Marissa kicked in unison. The top fence rail went flying.

"Yes!" T and Marissa high-fived, and Ben jumped over the remaining slats to grab the loose pipe. He picked it up and swung it like a baseball bat, hitting an imaginary ball far into the night air. He shaded his eyes as if watching it soar over the stadium fence.

They went back to the road and used the metal pole to extend the lug wrench. Now was the moment of truth. "Do you want to do the honors?" Ben asked Marissa. "It was your idea."

"I mean, T remembered where the fence was . . ."

T shook his head. "Nah, go for it. Come on, we got a tire to change!"

"Okay," she said. "Cross your fingers."

It worked like a charm. The second Marissa put pressure on the extended lug wrench, she could feel the difference. "Oh, my god, it's moving. You guys, it's working." The lug nut loosened under the wrench. "Leverage! Boom!" Marissa couldn't stop grinning. She did the magic trick on all five lug nuts and all of them came free.

Ben pumped his fists in the air, and T hugged Marissa around the shoulders.

She laughed in relief. "Oh, my god, you guys. I seriously thought we were going to have to lock ourselves in the car tonight and hope for some non-serial killer to come and help us."

At that moment Ben coughed awkwardly. The words came tumbling out. "I have to tell you something." He paused and looked at both of them to make sure he had their full attention. T gave him a nod of encouragement.

Ben swallowed hard. "Marissa, you were right. It was actually my fault."

"What was that?" She put a hand to her ear. "Could you just say that a little louder? I don't think I heard you. Did you say that I was right, and you were . . . wrong?"

"No, listen, I'm being serious," he said. "Do you want me to put it on tape? T, record this if you must: I messed up."

"Wait," said Marissa, and frowned. "What do you mean?"

Ben sighed. "My grandma asked me to do a bunch of car stuff before the trip, and one of them was to check the air pressure in the tires. And I didn't, and I'm pretty sure that's why the tire blew. It was my fault, and I'm sorry." He braced himself for her reaction.

But Marissa just studied his face for a minute, and then shook her head. "Don't worry about it."

He raised his eyebrows in surprise. "What?"

"I mean, I'm not going to lie, this is not how I wanted to spend our evening," said Marissa as a small smile appeared on her face. "But I really appreciate you fessing up. And, honestly, who knew tire pressure was such a big deal?"

"Well, I guess my grandma did," he said, and laughed tentatively.

T stepped in. "Okay, guys, it's . . ." He

paused to check his phone. "Seven thirty-five. We aren't that far from the festival site. We may have to sleep in the car tonight, but maybe we can still make the show. Let's get this baby on the road and get rolling!"

They jacked up the car again. From there it was easy to wiggle off the blown tire and get the spare one in its place.

As they were tightening the lug nuts on the spare, they saw a glimmer of headlights coming down the road. A car was coming their way. They all looked at each other, laughing a little nervously as they remembered Marissa's comment about the serial killer. T quickly finished securing the last lug nut as a pickup truck pulled onto the gravel just behind them. Ben started gathering up all the tools so that they could repack the car.

The other driver didn't turn off their lights, so it was hard to make out any details as a bulky silhouette hopped down from the cab. The figure approached them and stepped into the light, and Marissa sighed with relief. It was a middle-aged woman with short gray hair. She wore sensible jeans and a work jacket with a patch they recognized: "McCoy's Tire Repair."

The woman came over and introduced herself as Barb McCoy. "Maybe you saw my shop down the way? I always like to check the roads after a big gulley-washer like the one this afternoon. It's not unusual to have tire trouble after a storm like that, especially in this heat."

Marissa raised her eyebrows at Ben and laughed. "Thank you so much for coming by," she told Barb. "We could have used your help about an hour ago, but I think we got it all figured out. We're just trying to make it to the music festival down the road."

"Oh, that's right. It's starting tonight, is it?" She came over to their car. "Here, I'll check your spare."

Barb inspected their tires as Marissa nervously looked at the time and T and Ben repacked their things. She used her own wrench to check that the lug nuts were back on securely and then straightened up. "You kids did a good job on this!" she said. "Just be sure not to drive too far on the donut, okay? I'll give you my card if you want me to order you a replacement. I can have it ready in time for your drive back."

They took turns thanking her politely.

"Well, we'd better get going if we're going to make it to the show. It's her favorite singer," T said, nodding toward Marissa.

Barb headed back to her pickup. "All right, well, you kids drive safely! It's only about twenty minutes down the road. You can probably still make it."

As they pulled back onto the road, Ben burst into an off-key song. T and Marissa weren't even mad.

8:40 p.m.

Marissa leaned her head on T's shoulder in exhausted, happy relief. She'd been playing this moment in her head all year long, and it was finally happening. They were front and center for Natalia Chavez! Okay, well, far-left and toward the back. But still: they'd made it! Ben had driven the rest of the way to the festival and they'd pulled into the campsite just as Natalia's openers were finishing up.

The sun had completely disappeared behind the hills in the distance and the palm trees cut a dramatic silhouette against the twilight sky. The night temperature had dropped to a practically comfortable eighty-five degrees. If it cooled off a little more, Marissa might even get to wear the cute jean jacket that she'd brought along.

T was texting his mom: *Made it!* A relieved smiley-face emoji was the closest he came to indicating that there had been any doubt.

Ben grinned at Marissa. "See, not bad, right? Think it was all worth it?"

"As if I ever doubted!" Marissa elbowed T and shot him a *back-me-up-here* look, and both of them burst out laughing.

The lights went up on the main stage and the crowd roared with excitement. The familiar strains of "¡Baila, Baila . . . !" started up, and Natalia Chavez stepped onto the stage. Marissa looked at her friends with a beaming smile. "You guys, we did it!" she yelled, and the band began to play.

ABOUT THE AUTHOR

Elizabeth Neal lives in Columbus, OH, with her husband and daughter. They have a rescue dog who enjoys couch parkour, grumbling in her sleep, and things that squeak.